AR = 2.6
Lexile = 290

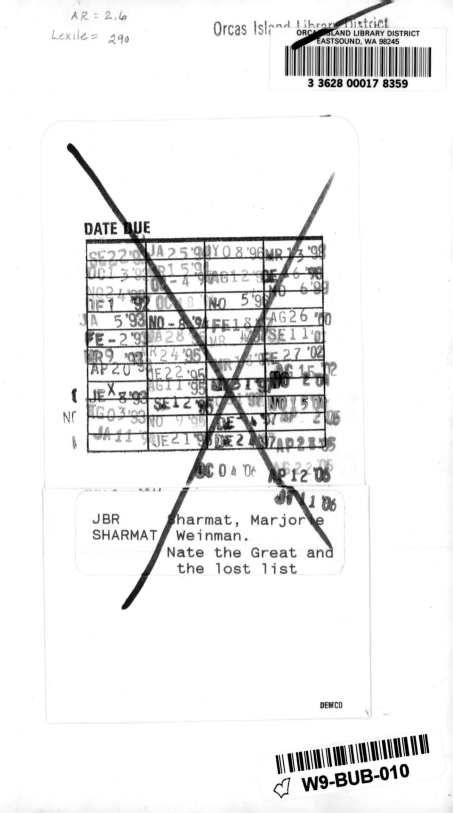

DEMCO

W9-BUB-010

A Break-of-Day Book

Ever since 1928, when Wanda Gág's classic *Millions of Cats* appeared, Coward-McCann has been publishing books of high quality for young readers. Among them are the easy-to-read stories known as Break-of-Day books. This series appears under the colophon shown above — a rooster crowing in the sunrise — which is adapted from one of Wanda Gág's illustrations for *Tales from Grimm*.

Though the language used in Break-of-Day books is deliberately kept as clear and as simple as possible, the stories are not written in a controlled vocabulary. And while chosen to be within the grasp of readers in the primary grades, their content is far-ranging and varied enough to captivate children who have just begun crossing the momentous threshold into the world of books.

Nate the Great
and the
Lost List

by

Marjorie Weinman Sharmat

illustrations by Marc Simont

COWARD-McCANN, INC.

New York

13   15   17   19   20   18   16   14   12

for someone special,
my cousin Rhoda

I, Nate the Great,
am a busy detective.
One morning I was not busy.
I was on my vacation.
I was sitting under a tree
enjoying the breeze
with my dog, Sludge,
and a pancake.
He needed a vacation too.
My friend Claude

7

came into the yard.

I knew that he

had lost something.

Claude was always losing things.

"I lost my way to your house,"

he said. "And then I found it."

"What else did you lose?"

"I lost the grocery list

I was taking to the store.

Can you help me find it?"

"I, Nate the Great,

am on my vacation," I said.

"When will your vacation be over?"

"At lunch."

"I need the list before lunch,"
Claude said.

"Very well. I, Nate the Great,
will take your case.
Tell me, what was on the list?"

"If I could remember, I wouldn't
need the list," Claude said.

"Good thinking," I said.

"Does anyone know what
was on the list?"

"My father," Claude said.

"He wrote it."

"Good. Can you find your father?"

"No, he won't be home
until lunch."

"Can you remember
some of the list?"

"Yes," Claude said. "I remember
salt, milk, butter, flour,
sugar, and tuna fish."

"Now, tell me, where did you
lose the list?"

"If I knew, I could
find it," Claude said.

"You can't be sure
of that," I said.

"What streets did you walk on?"

"I'm not sure," Claude said.

"I lost my way a few times."

"Then I, Nate the Great,
know what to do.
I will draw a map
of every street
between your house
and the grocery store
and we will follow the map."
Sludge and I got up.
Our vacation was over.

I got two pieces of paper
and a pen.
I drew a map
on one piece of paper.

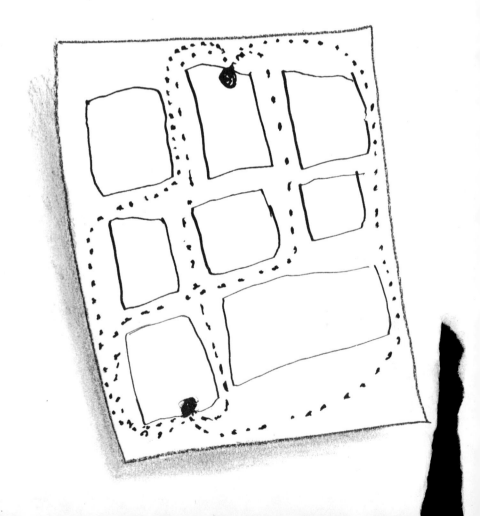

I wrote on the other:

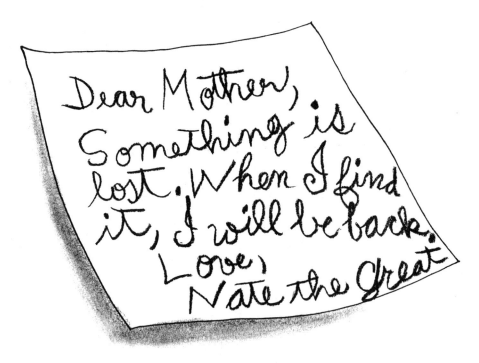

Dear Mother,
Something is
lost. When I find
it, I will be back.
Love,
Nate the Great

Claude said,
"I will walk with you."
"Don't get lost," I said,
"or I will have
two cases to solve."
We walked between Claude's house

and the grocery store
and then between the grocery store
and Claude's house.
Sludge sniffed.
But we could not find the list.
"Perhaps it blew away," I said.
I dropped the map
to the ground.
"What are you doing?"
Claude asked.
"I am dropping the map.
Whichever direction it goes
will show us the way
the wind is blowing.
Perhaps your list blew
in the same direction."

The map blew toward Rosamond's
house and disappeared.
"I will go
to Rosamond's house," I said.
"I will ask her if
she has seen your list."

"I will go to my house
and wait," Claude said.
"We are in front
of your house," I said.
"Yes, that makes it
easy to find," Claude said.

Sludge and I went
to Rosamond's house.
Rosamond opened the door.
Rosamond is a very strange girl.
Today she looked
more than strange.
She looked strange and white.
She was covered with flour.
Sludge sniffed hard.
I sniffed hard.
Rosamond smelled terrific.
Pancakes!
She was making pancakes.
We walked in.
Rosamond's four black cats
were there.

Today they were white, too.

The cats looked at Sludge.

They were not afraid of him.

Nobody is afraid of Sludge.

"I am making cat-pancakes

for my cats," Rosamond said,

"from a new recipe."

"I would like to taste

cat pancakes," I said.

"You are not a cat," Rosamond said.
"I would like to
taste them anyway," I said.
"A pancake is a pancake."
Rosamond and I sat down.
I ate a pancake.
It tasted fishy.
I ate another.

It tasted fishier.

"I am looking for Claude's grocery list," I said. "I think the wind blew it toward your house. Have you seen it?"

"I haven't seen a grocery list," Rosamond said. "But—"

"But what?"

"But I see Annie

and her dog, Fang,
outside my window, and—"
"And what?"
"And Fang has a piece of
paper in his mouth.
It might be the grocery list."

I got up.

"Thank you for your help
and your pancakes," I said.

"I am having a cat-pancake party
this morning," Rosamond said.

"I have invited
all the cats I know.

Can you come?"

"I am not a cat," I said.

24

"That's what I told
you before," Rosamond said.
Sludge and I went out
to talk to Annie and Fang.
I like Annie.
I try to like Fang.
"Hello," I said. "I am looking
for Claude's grocery list,
and I think Fang has found it.

25

It's between his teeth."
"He won't let
that paper go," Annie said.
"Can you pull it out?" I asked.
"No," Annie said.
"Fang would get mad."
"I would not like to see
Fang mad," I said.
"I, Nate the Great, say
that we should keep anybody
with sharp teeth happy.
Very happy."
I had a problem.
How could I get the paper
out of Fang's mouth?
Suddenly I had the answer.

"Sludge," I said. "Bark!"
Sludge barked.
Sludge barks funny.
But that does not matter.
Fang barked back.
The piece of paper
dropped from his mouth.
I reached for it.

But the wind blew it
down the street.
I went after it.
Sludge went after me.
Fang went after Sludge.

Annie went after Fang.

The paper went around the corner.

I went around the corner.

Sludge went around the corner.

Fang went around the corner.

Annie went around the corner.

The paper blew
into a fence.

I grabbed the paper.

The case was almost over.

I looked at the paper.

I saw many lines.

The paper was my map.

"The list is still lost," I said.
"I need more clues."
I thanked Annie and Fang
for their help.
Sludge and I
walked to Claude's house.
Claude was home.
He was not lost.
It was a good sign.
"I, Nate the Great, have not
found your list," I said.
"Can you remember anything else
that was written on it?"
"How will that help
you find it?" Claude asked.
"Trust me," I said.

"I remember! I remember
two more things," Claude said.
"Eggs and baking powder."
"Very good," I said.
"Can you find the list
before lunch?" Claude asked.
"I hope so," I said.

"Come to my house at eleven."
Sludge and I walked home slowly.
This was a hard case. At home
I made myself some pancakes.
I mixed eggs, flour, salt,
baking powder, milk, butter,
and sugar together and cooked them.

I gave Sludge a bone.

I ate and thought.

I thought about the grocery list.

I thought about Rosamond
and her fishy cat-pancakes.

I thought about Annie and Fang
and the map.

I put ideas together.

I took them apart.

Then I had a big idea.

I knew I must go back to
Rosamond's house.

I did not want to do that.

I did not want to be
at a party with Rosamond
and all the cats she knew.

But I had a job to do.
I had a case to solve.
Sludge and I walked quickly to
Rosamond's house.

I said hello to Rosamond
and more cats
than I could count.
They were all over
Rosamond's floor,

36

Rosamond's tables,
Rosamond's chairs,
and Rosamond.
"I came to talk about
your cat-pancakes," I said.
"Would you like more?"
Rosamond asked.
"I would like to see
your recipe," I said.
"Here it is," Rosamond said.
"There are no directions
in this recipe," I said.
"I don't need any," Rosamond said.
"I just mix
some of everything together."
"Tell me, where did you

get this recipe?"

"I found it today," Rosamond said.

"Aha! You found it," I said.

"Did you find it

near your house?"

"Yes," Rosamond said.

"How did you know that?"

"I have something to tell you.

I, Nate the Great, say that
your cat-pancake recipe
is Claude's grocery list."
I stood tall.
I cleared my throat.
I read the recipe.
"Salt
milk
butter
flour
tuna fish
eggs
baking powder
sugar
salmon
liver."

"Oh," Rosamond said.
"When I found the paper,
I thought it was a
cat-pancake recipe."

"Yes," I said. "And when I
saw Fang holding a piece of paper,
I thought it was a grocery list.
I thought it was what I
hoped it was.

When you saw the grocery list,
you thought it was
what you hoped it was.
A cat-pancake recipe.

I, Nate the Great, thought of that
when I was making pancakes.
I mixed eggs, flour, salt,
baking powder, milk, butter,
and sugar.
Claude had told me they
were on his list.
The other thing he remembered
on the list was tuna fish.
Cats like tuna fish.
So—cat pancakes!"

"Oh," Rosamond said.
"Well, Claude
can have his paper back.
I will keep the recipe
in my head."
"That is a good place for it,"
I said. "It cannot blow away."
I said good-bye to Rosamond
and more cats
than I could count.

Sludge and I went home
with the list.
The case was solved.
And it was almost eleven o'clock.
When Claude comes at eleven,
I will give him his list.

It is now past eleven o'clock.
It is now past eleven-thirty.
Claude has not shown up.
I do not see him anywhere.
I hope Claude has not lost
himself.

It is now past twelve.

Here comes Claude.

I am glad I do not have
to look for him.

I am glad the case is over.

I, Nate the Great,
have something important to do.

I, Nate the Great,
am going to finish
my vacation.